A dragon called
Môr

*Dedicated to the children
and staff of Tŷ Hafan
and to Joe and Lewis,
the most honest critics in the whole of Wales.*

A dragon called Môr

Jilly Bebbington

y Lolfa

Thanks to Prof. Gwynedd Pierce and Aled Islwyn
for editing, translating and encouragement.

Thanks for donations from Three Arches Garage,
Three Arches pub, Medi-Optics, businesses in Rhydypennau,
Clearwater and Maryport, Sound Women (Penarth)
and friends and family.

First impression: 2020
© Jilly Bebbington & Y Lolfa Cyf., 2020
© Pictures: Andrea Grealy

Cover design: Y Lolfa
Cover picture / illustration: Andrea Grealy

ISBN: 978 1 78461 799 8

Published and printed in Wales
on paper from well-maintained forests by
Y Lolfa Cyf., Talybont, Ceredigion SY24 5HE
e-mail ylolfa@ylolfa.com
website www.ylolfa.com
tel 01970 832 304
fax 832 782

Contents

1
A dragon called Môr

Môr was a young dragon who lived in the Severn Sea. That's how he got his name, his full name being Môr Hafren, the Welsh name for the Severn Sea.

He was a gentle dragon, but he was full of fun, a vegetarian and an intellectual (that means he was very bright). While he loved playing in the waves and bouncing and sliding on sandbanks, he was rather lonely.

You can't play Tag on your own – it's not as much fun as playing with a friend. He had a cousin called Haf, but she lived in Somerset, or Gwlad yr Haf, so he didn't get to see her very often. They were both young dragons and had not yet learnt to fly. They could swim as well as the fishes in the sea, but their wings were not strong enough to fly. It would be some months before they could take to the air as fully-fledged flying dragons.

One windy autumn evening Môr was playing in the white horse waves close to Sully. He dived through one particularly large wave and a gust of wind blew him onto the rocks. He bumped his ribs and tummy rather badly. It quite took his breath away, so he decided to climb onto the shore for a breather. By now it was quite dark and the clouds were covering the moon, so it wasn't very easy to see.

He saw some lights just a little way from the sea. He crawled up the bank, through a fence and across the garden until he was quite close to the lights. He looked into a room and could see children laughing as they watched a cartoon. They seemed to be having fun, and Môr felt lonelier than ever.

He moved to the next window and saw blue water. This water did not have windy waves like the sea but was flat and still. Môr wondered what it was. He moved on to the next window. This room was dark except for a nightlight and somebody was asleep in bed, so Môr moved on again to the next window.

A young girl was lying on the bed, close to a wheelchair. She was awake but looked a little sad, Môr thought. He decided to introduce himself. He could speak both Welsh and English, so he tapped very gently on the window with his claw,

"Excuse me, *esgusodwch fi,*" he asked, "may I come in?"

The little girl jumped at the sight of him but got herself into the wheelchair and rolled it over to the window.

"Are you REALLY a DRAGON?"

"Yes, my name is Môr."

"I'm Lisa," said the girl. "Come in, if you can!"

"That's easy," said Môr. "Dragons can fit through quite narrow spaces."

"So I see!" Lisa said.

They looked at each other for quite a long time.

"You're very handsome," said Lisa.

Môr blushed pink under his blue skin, and said, "And you're pretty. What is that carriage you're riding in?"

"It's called a wheelchair. I use it because my legs don't work very well. It's electric – see?"

"Wow – I'm impressed. That's cool! Can I have a go?"

"Yes," said Lisa, "but you'll have to sit on my lap. I'll show you how it works."

They had a great time for the next few minutes whizzing round the room, with Môr getting to understand and work the controls.

"This is fun!" said Môr. "I was lonely out at sea, and the wind is all mournful and blowing really hard tonight. It's good

to have company and someone to talk to."

"I couldn't agree more, Môr," giggled Lisa. "I couldn't get off to sleep and my carer has gone for a break to the Cwtsh, because she thought I was asleep. She'll be back soon and she won't believe her eyes if she sees you."

"I don't think she'll see me," said Môr thoughtfully. "Most grown-ups can't see me. You have to BELIEVE in dragons to be able to see me. Actually, I'll have to get back to that rather cold sea soon, because sea dragons' skins dry out quickly, but I'd rather stay here with you and talk."

"I know what we'll do!" said Lisa. "We can go to our pool. The water's heated and you can swim as much as you like.

I'll come in too – if you can help me with my swimming costume. It'll be quite safe for me to go in with a good swimmer like you."

"Way to go!" said Môr. "We can have a great time together!"

And they did. Môr helped Lisa and they swam in the warm pool. Lisa rode on Môr's back and they enjoyed themselves hugely. At last Lisa thought that they had better get back to her room in case her carer was wondering where she had got to.

"I've had a lovely time," said Môr. "May I come again?"

"Of course! Next time you can play with the other children. I'm only here for a few days. Mum and Dad and my brother are staying in the flat upstairs but I'll be back in a few weeks and we can play together again. I've so enjoyed our time together."

"What's this place called?" asked Môr.

"It's called Tŷ Hafan," said Lisa, "and we come here for a break and a good time. We have lots of fun, and lovely food. Oh, by the way, most of the Play Team believe in dragons — they'll be able to play with us too. It'll be our secret for now."

"Great," said Môr. "I needn't be lonely any more — I know where to come now. Bye!"

And with that he left, walked to the shore and swam away.

Lisa went to sleep straight away because she was happy-tired.

"Oh… sleeping like a baby," said her

carer in a little while, "and smiling as if she's really happy. I wonder why her hair is a bit damp — it's almost as if she's been swimming!"

Môr swam out to sea and he too was happy.

"I don't have to be lonely any more — I can always go to Tŷ Hafan and play with the children there!"

2
Môr and the
Cookery Club

Môr was swimming in the sea just outside Tŷ Hafan. He was floating on his back, blowing fountains of water into the air and watching them flow back into the sea. Then he whipped them up with his tail until they were froth. He enjoyed mixing the water.

"Môr!" Lisa called, on the lawn in the Tŷ Hafan garden. "Come and play with us, please?"

"Be right with you – *mewn munud*," said Môr.

Quickly he swam to the rocky shore, clambered up and through the fence.

"Hello, all!" said Môr.

Robyn, Wyn, Lisa and Rhys were in their wheelchairs in the garden.

Now, you will remember that Môr could only be seen by people who believe in dragons. Of course Lisa, Wyn, Robyn and Rhys all believed and so did their carers, Gareth, Mai and Candice. Gigi, Robyn's carer, was not a believer.

"Oh, they just exist in fairy stories, but it would be nice if there really were real dragons," Gigi said wistfully.

"You've got to believe or you won't ever see him," Robyn told her.

Gigi was still unsure, but she did notice that the special swing that Lisa and Rhys had their wheelchairs on, was moving rapidly back and forth. Gigi could see a dim outline of something with a faint hint of blue pushing the swings.

"Well, it's nearly time for the Cookery Club, just five more minutes!" called Candice. The swing swung wildly to squeaks of delight from both Rhys and Lisa.

Jane, from the kitchen, came to the door to the garden and popped her head out.

"Julia, Dave and I have finished clearing up after lunch, so you can all come in for the Cookery Club now," she called. "Julia's baking and icing cupcakes!"

Môr stopped pushing and thought, "How can you makes cakes out of cups? Sounds a bit indigestible to me!"

Being of an enquiring nature, he was determined to find out more before he gave final judgement.

The gang and their carers went into the hospice and over to the kitchen, where Julia put aprons and chef's hats on them and saw that they washed their hands carefully. Môr watched from beside the dishwasher rather nervously.

"I'm vegetarian – I don't eat cups," he informed Julia.

"Oh, that's just the shape of the cakes," Julia told him. "The cakes are made of flour, eggs, butter and sugar as usual. When they're made, we'll ice them with chocolate icing, which we'll prepare while the cakes cool."

Môr was still a little dubious and stayed

sheltering by the dishwasher. He was pleased, however, that all the kitchen staff could see him, which meant that they believed in dragons.

The children mixed the cake mixture with a special gadget. They only had to touch a huge button for the mixer to work. Julia even persuaded Môr to put a claw on the button and he laughed to see how easily it worked. Everybody had a turn at working the mixture.

Julia popped the cakes in the oven. They only took ten minutes to cook in the little paper cases. Môr was fascinated by the big oven. His eyes grew huge as the door opened and he could feel the heat coming out.

"When I grow up and can fly and make

fire, I'll be able to cook cakes all by myself!" he thought to himself.

"Here's the icing sugar and the cocoa powder for you to mix," announced Dave.

Môr moved closer to the worktop. He'd never seen icing sugar before so he was amazed at how fine the white powder looked.

"Have a taste, everyone," Julia said, as she gave everyone a little lick using tiny spoons.

Môr stuck his nose in quite far — too far, in fact. He felt a tickling sensation at the back of his throat and in his nose. He suddenly sneezed very hard and very loudly — right into the bowl of icing sugar! It flew everywhere and before you could say 'coals of fire' everybody and everything was covered in a fine coating of white dust. Jane was helpless with laughter, tears running down her cheeks as she looked at the surprised, VERY pale blue dragon. All the children and staff were shouting with laughter.

"*Bobol annwyl*, I'm so sorry!" said Môr.

"Never mind, we'll soon get this mess sorted out…" said Dave, "… when you've all finished laughing!"

As they tidied up, Gigi said, "Well, I didn't believe Môr existed before, but looking at this mess I'm now convinced he's real!"

They all settled down to eat the cupcakes (not made out of cups) and iced with a fresh batch of chocolate icing.

"What an adventurous day!" thought Môr.

3
Môr and the laundry

Môr was wandering up the corridor by the children's rooms at Tŷ Hafan. His friend Ifan was having a bath, and his carer, Tony, had gently suggested that there wasn't quite enough room for a growing dragon, as well as Ifan and the two carers, in the bathroom. Môr could take a hint and he went back into the corridor.

He could hear hammering and rather rude words coming up from further down the corridor. Being of a curious nature, he decided to investigate. He passed the

Cwtsh, but there was no one in there having a *cwtsh* or a cuddle.

"It's no good, I need a new part," said Jasper, who was looking rather sadly at the tumble dryer in the laundry room.

"Botheration! I've got all these towels to dry – we get through loads of them in the hospice every day, as you know, Môr." Carol was looking even sadder than Jasper.

Môr followed Jasper to the stores.

"I haven't got the right part here," said Jasper. "I'll have to order it online. It'll be here by tomorrow, but Carol needs that laundry done today. We can't dry it outside, it's raining buckets out there."

"It's raining *hen wragedd a ffyn*, as we say in Welsh – that means old ladies with their walking sticks," said Môr. "It's not going to clear up either. The weather forecast is awful for the rest of the day."

(Môr liked watching the weather forecast. 'Our Derek' would always let him know if it was going to be too stormy for Môr to swim far out to sea in the Môr Hafren outside the hospice.)

"It'll take ages for the towels to dry just hanging on a clothes horse. I'll have to think of something. You're a clever dragon – any ideas?"

"I've got a glimmer of an idea – it might work, but it might not. Let me think about it," said Môr and he headed back to the Cwtsh to have a think. He sat on the couch, carefully draping his tail over the arm and being very careful where he put his claws.

"I'm getting stronger as more people believe in me," he thought. "I can't fly yet, just jump about a bit; and I can't quite make fire yet — BUT I can huff hot air. THAT might help Carol. I know, I'll go to the kitchen and see if Jane and Julia have any more fresh ginger. It tastes warm and spicy and will make my breath smell nice."

Jane and Julia were only too happy to give Môr some root ginger.

"Yum!" exclaimed Môr, chomping happily on a large piece of root. "Stay calm and chew ginger!"

"What a funny little dragon he is," remarked Jane. "Fancy wanting to chew ginger! I wonder why?"

"There's always a reason with that little chap," said Julia. "He's quite a clever dragon, you know – and have you noticed he's not so little anymore? Our Môr is growing up."

Môr walked down the corridor, chewing like mad. He arrived back in the laundry room, hiccupping happily.

"I've had a – hic – idea!"

"What have you been eating?" asked Carol.

"Fresh ginger. It's hot – *poeth* – you see."

"No, I don't see," replied Carol.

"Well, you know that dragons can breathe fire?" said Môr.

"YOU'RE NOT BREATHING FIRE OVER MY CLEAN TOWELS!" cried Carol. "You'd singe them, and you'd set off the fire alarm and maybe burn down the laundry room. It doesn't bear thinking about!"

"I can't actually breathe fire yet," said Môr. "Only hot air."

"You're full of hot air! Now I think about it, that could be useful – are you sure there are no flames?"

"Positive. It's just a matter of burping after eating something warming like ginger. I'd need to eat butter or some oil to make flames and I haven't done that," reassured Môr.

"Well, we could give it a go," said Carol.

So they did.

Carol arranged the towels on racks and Môr burped politely, breathing warm, ginger-smelling air all over them. They began to steam and then dry.

It took some time, and several refills of ginger, but eventually Carol declared that twenty five towels were now dry and aired.

That was enough towels to be getting on with until her tumble dryer was fixed by Jasper the following morning.

"Thank you, Môr dear!" exclaimed Carol. "You've saved my bacon."

"But I'm a vegetarian!" said Môr. "I don't DO bacon! I like laverbread rolled in oats for my breakfast!"

"It's just an expression, Môr," explained Carol. "It means that you've helped me very much and now the children will have clean, dry and aired towels. Môr, you are a sweet, good little dragon and I love you."

"I'm not so little any more," said Môr, and indeed it did seem as if he had grown a few centimetres in the last few hours.

★

Ifan had finished having his bath, was dried with fresh warm towels and he, and the slightly bigger Môr, had an enjoyable time playing percussion instruments in the music room with Diane, the music therapist. Later on, they blew bubbles which were ENORMOUS and popped with a strong smell of ginger as Môr used up the last of his hot air.

"I DO love you, Môr," said Ifan. "You are the nicest dragon in the whole world."

Môr grew another couple of centimetres and beamed happily at Ifan.

"I love you, too," he said.

4
Môr goes to Touch Trust

Annette, from the Play Team, was in the Activity Room at Tŷ Hafan with two of the children (Philip with Mai, and Jason with Beth) when she heard a tap on the outside door.

"Well hello, Môr," she said. "How are you today? Have you come to play?"

"Yes, please," said Môr. "Can I do something to help?"

"Of course you can, Môr," Annette said. "We're making hand and foot prints to use in craft work. You can help by painting Philip's hand and foot ready for printing."

"Great," replied Môr. "What colour?"

"Well, we're using green, because we need lots of prints to make a jungle background to display on the walls by the Cwtsh. When we've got enough, we can put in the jungle animals."

"Are there DRAGONS in the jungle?" asked Môr.

"Well, there are tigers and monkeys, and parrots in the sky," answered Annette. "I don't see why we can't put in dragons, too!"

Môr looked pleased. He was very dexterous (handy) with his claws and could hold a paintbrush very well. He carefully put green paint on Philip's hand and foot.

"Now we'll print lots of them," said Mai.

"Thank you, Môr," said Annette. "Can you help Mai to wash the paint off now? In ten minutes I'm going down to the Sensory Room to have a Touch Trust session. Do you want to come and help with blowing warm air and playing percussion instruments with us?"

"Yes, please. *Diolch yn fawr*," replied Môr enthusiastically. "I'll go and get a piece of ginger to chew to make warm air. I'll be with you in ten minutes."

Annette, Philip with Mai, Jason with Beth and Anwen with Eleri were all outside the Sensory Room when Môr trundled up the corridor.

"*Poeth!*" he remarked. "Hot!"

"Come on, Môr, we'll position the beanbags for the children while the carers lift them out of the wheelchairs."

They arranged the beanbags and the children laid down on them with their carers nearby.

"You can lie down on the waterbed, Môr," said Annette.

"It'll remind you of the sea – *Môr ar y môr*," joked Eleri, as she made sure that Anwen was comfortable on her beanbag.

"Everybody settled? The lights are going down." Annette and the carers clapped a welcome to the dark and to each other. "We're going to start by tapping these Tibetan bells," continued Annette. "If you can tap them, fine, but if not, Môr will give you a hand – or rather, a claw!"

Môr's eyes shone brightly with delight. Then Annette played gentle music, which was very relaxing, and the carers gave gentle massage to the children. They were all chilled out. Môr was good at this and also surprisingly good at keeping quiet too.

"Lights up and let's see what noises we can make with the percussion," said Annette.

Neither Jason nor Anwen could move a great deal, so Môr, Beth and Eleri helped them to make noises using the percussion instruments.

"A big clap for you all," said Annette. "You did so well! Now we'll get out the soft materials. Can you help please, Môr?"

The carers chose fabrics made of silk, muslin, taffeta and sparkly sequinned material.

"We'll move these fabrics gently over the children, so that they can feel their different qualities. Môr, can you blow the materials?" asked Annette.

"Great! *Bendigedig!*" replied Môr, burping happily in a ginger sort of way. "My hot air is good today!"

"Not too hot, Môr! We don't want to melt the silk!" exclaimed Annette.

"OK, cool!" muttered Môr.

"Exactly," said Annette crisply.

Everyone enjoyed the feel of the materials blowing over their skin and they all clapped as their carers watched for the slightest movements of the children's reactions.

"I'm not actually very good at clapping," said Môr sadly. "I have trouble with my claws."

"We all have some trouble reacting," comforted Eleri. "Many of the children can't move very well – but we all try, which is the important thing. *Da iawn*, Môr. Well done!"

"So we'll have some relaxing music with the lights turned down," and Annette turned on the music, which sounded like the sea, and the Magic Carpet showed slow-moving fishes floating on the floor as if they were on a seabed, with fronds of seaweed waving in calming patterns.

They were all feeling relaxed and

happy – but some were more relaxed than others.

There was a gentle sound coming from Môr's waterbed. Môr was snoring in a haze of warm ginger. Everybody smiled

to see a happy, snoring little dragon.

"I do love that little chap," said Annette softly. "He's such a kind, caring dragon – it seems a shame to wake him."

The children and their carers left Môr in the Sensory Room, with the bubble machine working gently. He was fast asleep, dreaming happy dreams.

5
Môr's busy day

Môr was stumping about Tŷ Hafan, enjoying himself. He'd gone swimming in the pool with Lisa and then helped the children make and decorate cards. He got very sticky and covered in glitter whilst making the cards.

After cleaning his claws, he visited the kitchen, where he sneaked some ginger from Julia, and he was now looking for something else to do.

Jodie was passing the Activity Room.

"Hi, Môr!" she said. "Are you looking for something to do? You can help me to shred some old papers if you like."

"Yes, great!" said Môr, enthusiastically. "The older children have gone to get ready for a trip. Paul is driving them to Barry Island – but that won't be for ages yet."

"Follow me, then," said Jodie and they walked to the office, with Môr flexing his little wings (which were slowly growing) as they went. "You can help me put this shredded paper into bags, Môr. There's so much of it, and it's quite expensive to get rid of in the paper recycling."

"Why don't I burn it with my flames?" said Môr.

"Pollution," said Ali and Nicki together in a chorus.

"Oh, my fire doesn't make any smoke," said Môr. "It just burns hot and pure."

"Are you sure, Môr?" asked Amanda.

"We don't want to pollute the air around Tŷ Hafan — or anywhere else for that matter," added Teresa.

"Oh, no, I don't DO pollution!" assured Môr. "My fire is special — and I've been trying it out a lot lately."

So they dragged out lots of bags of paper to the far end of the gardens, by the compost heaps and Jasper said that he would supervise. Môr went to the kitchen to get some vegetable oil to 'fuel his pipes', as he put it. They left Jodie and the gang to answer the phone and carry on with the office work and Môr very quickly, and cleanly, burnt the piles of shredded paper — leaving the bags for further use.

"My word, that little dragon is very

useful in many ways!" remarked Jasper to Jodie after he and Môr had tidied up in the garden. "He even put the ashes on the compost heap so that they can be recycled into the garden."

"Thank you so much for your help, Môr," said Jodie. "You're such a helpful dragon to have around the hospice."

Môr blushed pink under his blue scales. "I'm going to see Paul about the trip," he said. "I'm wondering if I can sit on the roof of the van?"

Paul was checking the state of the tyres, the screen-wash and the petrol in the Tŷ Hafan van when Môr arrived.

"No, you can't possibly travel on the roof!" Paul exclaimed. "It's a matter of health and safety. How would it look if I

was driving around in a van full of kids in wheelchairs, with a loose dragon on the roof? I'd lose my driving licence!"

"Oh," replied Môr in a disappointed sort of way. "I didn't think anyone would see me. And I could flex my wings on the way?"

"I bet the police believe in dragons," said Paul, rolling his eyes at Alex, who was supervising from his wheelchair. He was one of the older boys going on the trip. "Now, Môr, it really wouldn't be safe for us with you on top of the bus. You wouldn't want to cause an accident if someone had a fright seeing you!"

"Oh, I wouldn't want to cause any trouble like that!" exclaimed Môr.

Half an hour later Môr was inside the bus, with his safety-belt on and with Alex and two other teenagers with carers Paul, Sara and Tony, all seated firmly inside.

"Barry Island, here we come!" cried Alex and John.

Everyone laughed and Paul put some good music on the van's CD player.

Môr's eyes went wide with pleasure as they got to the amusement arcades at Barry Island. He could see flashing lights and all sorts of games to play. He discovered that he could play some games, but not others. He was a little hampered by his claws and by his funny shape. Some of the children were not faring much better. A few of the games were fine, but not all were designed for wheelchair-users or dragons.

After a while, Paul called everybody and suggested that they have ice-creams and candy floss.

"We'll all have to brush our teeth when we get back – it's all rather sugary!" he announced, as he gave his order.

Môr loved the ice-cream, even though he dropped a bit down his front.

"There's one extra candy floss. Are you having two, mate?" asked the man on the stall.

"No, one's enough for me!" replied Paul, realising that the man couldn't see Môr. The man obviously didn't believe in dragons and wiped his glasses quite hard when he saw Môr's candy floss apparently floating in the air and disappearing fast!

Môr was, by now, in rather a mess. He had ice-cream down his front, and his claws and teeth were sticking together with sugary goo.

"We'll have to clean you up before we take you in the van," said Paul, "or you'll stick to the seats."

"After all that *sothach* (junk food) I think I'd better swim back to Tŷ Hafan," said Môr. "The sea will clean me and I can chew some seaweed to clean my teeth."

Môr went down to the beach, charged into the sea and began to swim around the headland, back to Tŷ Hafan.

6
Môr to the rescue!

The wind was blustering around Ty Hafan, so Môr and the children and carers had to cut short their nature walk as the clouds were blowing in. They had watched the green woodpeckers digging for insects in the lawn by the trees and they had laughed at the antics of the herring gulls tumbling and playing in the wind. They just had time to smell some of the plants – Môr liked the rosemary, thyme and sage particularly.

"I'm a vegetarian, you see. *Clywch yr ogla.*"

'You don't LISTEN to smells in

English," teased Eleri. "But you do that in Welsh!"

"Time to go in, it's getting cold out here and the rain will come soon," said Tony.

They all trooped in, with Môr waggling his wings one last time before entering the hospice. Môr's wings were getting stronger but he had not even tried to fly yet. He just wasn't sure how strong his wings were and was rather nervous about TRYING to fly, truth be told. Môr was a little upset, because his cousin, Haf, could already fly and she was rather smug about her new ability.

There was a visitor in the hospice when they arrived in the lounge. Bailey, the PAT (Pets as Therapy) dog was there. Bailey was a Cavapoo dog (half Cavalier

Spaniel and half poodle) and visited the children at Tŷ Hafan on a regular basis. She was a friendly, gentle dog who loved being hugged and petted. She also loved to do tricks. She could pirouette on her hind legs, she rolled over and followed other commands like 'wag a tail'.

Her owner, Siân, had a bag with special toys for Bailey to play with – and Môr loved one of these. It was a special rubber toy that squeaked, but only Bailey could hear it, as its pitch was too high for humans to hear. Môr, however, had super hearing and could also hear the squeak. He loved helping the children to throw the squeaking toy for Bailey to fetch. All the children enjoyed her visit, as usual, and they were quite sad when Siân said that she and Bailey should be leaving, before the wind got any worse. So Bailey shook paws with everyone, including Môr, and off they went.

Then Russell, the clown, arrived and made wonderful models out of balloons, in whatever shapes the children asked of him. He warned Môr to be careful with his claws, because balloons pop easily. He needn't have bothered to warn Môr. Môr hated the bang when a balloon popped, so kept fearfully away from them altogether.

The children, carers and Môr were all settling down to watch a film (*How to Train your Dragon* – "Huh!" said Môr, disgustedly) when they suddenly heard a whoosh! and saw a red rocket going up in the sky next to the hospice. It came from the sea.

"*Beth ar y ddaear*? What on earth?"

"That's a distress rocket," said Paul, who was walking through the lounge on his way to the Activity Room.

"That means that someone is in trouble at sea," said Tony. "I'd better phone the Coastguard."

Everyone rushed to the window and from there they could see a yacht in the distance, with its mast blown right over and its sail flapping in the wind. The whole yacht was leaning over to starboard (right). A man was hanging onto the ropes and trying to right the boat, but he was not having much success.

"The Coastguards say that the Penarth

Lifeboat is out on another rescue," said Tony. "I'd better try Air Sea Rescue."

After a short interval Tony explained, "They can't get here for at least fifteen minutes, but they'll try their best."

"I don't think that boat will still be afloat in fifteen minutes time," said Paul worriedly. "The wind is a full gale now."

"I wish I could fly to help, but I'm frightened to try. Not everyone believes in dragons," whispered Môr nervously.

"You can do it, Môr!" said Lisa firmly. "Just think – you don't really need people to BELIEVE in you. You know that we all love you and you love us, don't you? It's LOVE that matters, you know. You can do it. That man needs you to rescue him."

"OK, I'll try," said Môr, sticking out his chest. "I'll do it for him – and for all of you."

Môr stepped out of the door onto the lawn. He took a short run and thought as he ran, "They all love me!" He flapped his wings and…

HE FLEW !

He circled the yacht at sea, swooped down and plucked the man from the waves with his strong claws. He lifted the man with all his strength, carried him carefully, despite the gale, and deposited him neatly on the lawn of Tŷ Hafan.

"Hooray for Môr!" cried everyone at Tŷ Hafan. "Oh, you clever dragon!"

The carers rushed out to help the man, who was not much the worse for wear,

and indeed was quite bouncy after a cup of tea and a biscuit.

"I don't know what picked me up and dumped me on the lawn," said the man. "It was rather like magic!"

"I think it was love that did the trick," said Lisa happily.

"Yes, love. *Ie, cariad*," thought Môr.